The Year Mom Won the Pennant

The Year Mom

Won the Pennant

Matt Christopher

Illustrations by FOSTER CADDELL

Little, Brown and Company

BOSTON   TORONTO   LONDON

Republished in 1986

The Library of Congress has cataloged this work as follows:

Christopher, Matt.

The year Mom won the pennant, [by] Matt Christopher. Illus. by Foster Caddell. [1st ed.] Boston, Little, Brown [1968]

147 p. illus. 20 cm.

Summary: The boys are all hesitant when one boy's mother is the only parent who volunteers to coach their Little League team, but there is quite a surprise in store for them.

[1. Baseball—Fiction] I. Caddell, Foster, illus. II. Title.

PZ7.C458 Ye   [Fic]   68-11110

MARC

ISBN 0-316-13954-8   AC
ISBN 0-316-13988-2 (pbk)

HC: 10 9

PB: 10 9

VB

Published simultaneously in Canada
by Little, Brown & Company (Canada) Limited

Printed in the United States of America

To
Charlie Foote

The Year Mom Won the Pennant

1

NICK VASSEY drilled the ball straight over the plate. *Boom!* The ball connected solidly with Gale Matson's bat and rocketed over the fence, far left of the foul line.

"Quit pulling that ball!" yelled Cyclone Maylor at second base.

"I'm not pulling it!" Gale yelled back, his face glistening in the hot sun. "I'm hitting it!"

Nick grinned. In spite of the monkey business going on, Gale could make the most sour-looking puss break into a smile.

A moment later the smile disappeared. "Isn't anybody going after that ball?" Nick asked.

No one budged. The outfielders and the infielders were standing like statues, some of them with their arms crossed, some even with their ankles crossed.

Pat Krupa, standing near third base, was closest to the ball.

"Go after it, will you, Pat?" pleaded Nick. "We don't have many balls."

Pat glanced at the others behind him, made a face, and went on a slow run after the ball. He had to go out the gate, then swing right behind the fence. "Straighten 'em out next time," he grumbled as he ran by.

This is the trouble when you don't have a coach, thought Nick. No one wants to do anything extra.

Jerry Wong, who was catching the balls

4

thrown in from the fielders, tossed him a ball. Nick stretched and aimed a pitch at the outside corner. Gale swung and drove the ball inches past Nick's right ear.

"Hey! What have I done to you? Okay, lay this one down, Gale."

Gale bunted the next pitch down the third-base line and beelined for first. Jim Rennie batted next. Finally they all had taken their turns. But Wayne Snow wanted to bat again.

"If you do, everybody else will want to," said Nick. "And we've got to have outfield and infield practice."

"We can have outfield and infield practice the next time," argued Wayne. "Come on, somebody. Pitch to me."

"I'll pitch a couple to you if you'll pitch a couple to me," offered Tom Warren, the team's best hitter last year.

"You're on," said Wayne.

"Who's going to shag them?" snapped Scotty Page. "*I'm* not."

Nick looked from one to the other and began to feel wretched. You can't have a team with each guy wanting his own way. It would fall apart in no time.

"You know what's going to happen?" Gale Matson piped up. "There won't be a Thunderballs team, that's what. Not unless we get a coach."

"But Nick says his father doesn't want to coach us any more," Jim Rennie said.

"Why not?" Cyclone turned a surprised look at Nick.

Nick shrugged. "He's working later hours now, so he doesn't have time. And he's never won the pennant. He figures maybe someone else could do better. How about your father, Gale? Have you asked him?"

"He's a cop," Gale answered. "He works different shifts. He can't."

"My dad can't either," said Cyclone. "He's a pilot. He's away a lot."

"How about your dad, Wayne?" Nick asked. "Think he'd like to coach us?"

Wayne shook his head and ran his hand up the full length of his bat. "He doesn't have time either."

"Looks as if the Thunderballs have just fallen apart," announced Russell Gray. "I'm going to get on another team before it's too late."

"It *is* too late," said Nick. "The other teams have been formed."

"Then what are we going to do?"

"I don't know," said Nick.

"You sure, Dad?" Nick pleaded again while Mom and the girls, Jen and Sue, were placing the food on the table. "Are you sure you won't have time to coach this year?"

"I'm sure," replied Dad. "I've told you my reasons, Nick. I'm working more hours. And I've coached the team for four years and have never come close to first place. Give some other father a chance. Maybe he can do better."

"But no other father *wants* to coach us, Dad," exclaimed Nick. "They all have excuses, too. And without a coach, we won't have a team!"

Jen and Sue sat down at their regular places across from Nick, and Mom was across from Dad. After Dad said grace, they began eating. Hamburg, mashed potatoes and corn usually would make Nick forget everything else for a while. But this time the fate of the Thunderballs was uppermost in his mind. What would he do all summer if he didn't play baseball?

"Guess there just won't be any Thunderballs this year," Jen said, putting a forkful of potatoes into her mouth. Her voice, thought Nick, sounded like the knell of doom.

"I have a thought," Mom said.

Nick's ears perked up. "What, Mom? That I play on another team? I can't. It's too late."

"No. Not that."

"What, then, Mom?"

Mom's eyes twinkled. "Okay if I tried it? Coaching the Thunderballs, I mean?"

Nick stared at her. "You? You coach the Thunderballs? Is that what you said, Mom?"

Mom smiled. "That's what I said."

2

"BUT, Mom!" Nick was dumbfounded. "What do you know about coaching? And who ever heard of a woman coaching a baseball team?"

Mom loved baseball just as much as Dad. But only as a spectator. She just *couldn't* mean what she had said.

"I've watched baseball games for more years than I'd care to mention," Mom explained. "And I've seen coaches work too. Particularly your father."

"And I bet Mom can do just as well," Sue put in, shaking back her blond curls.

Her smile showed where she had lost a tooth.

"She just might do better," Dad admitted, beaming.

"She just might," echoed Jen, who had been born between Nick and Sue.

"What have you got to lose?" Dad said. "Without her you might not have a team at all. With her you will."

Nick shrugged. He wasn't exactly elated about the idea. "Well, I guess having a team is better than not having one," he agreed. "Even if we don't win a single game."

"Thanks for the compliment," said Mom.

Nick squeezed out a grin. "I'm sorry, Mom. I really didn't mean that. You sure you want to coach us?"

"Yes, I'm sure. But first you'd better ask

your teammates if it's all right with them."

"Wait till tomorrow, Nick," suggested Dad. "This evening you call all the guys and tell them there's practice tomorrow. Tomorrow Mom goes with you to the park and tells the boys she's your new coach. If they don't like it they might as well forget about having a team."

Nick was glum. He had never heard of a woman coach. Never. The guys wouldn't go for it in a million years.

At six o'clock the next afternoon every member of the Thunderballs baseball team was present at the field. So was Mom. Most of the boys knew her. Nick introduced her to the few boys she didn't know.

Mom's talk to the boys was brief. She said that Nick had told her that the Thun-

derballs had trouble getting a coach this year, that it was impossible for Mr. Vassey to coach them for a couple of good reasons, and that she had volunteered.

"Some of you might have doubts about my coaching because I'm a woman," she added. "If you do, think of all the women

in positions today whom men had doubts about years ago. And I do happen to know of women coaching basketball and softball. There's no doubt that women are coaching baseball in some other parts of the country." She paused to let that thought sink into their heads a bit. "At least, if I coach, we'll have a team. Isn't it better than not to play at all? Well, what do I hear? Will you accept me as coach? Or won't you?"

There was silence for a second. A long second. It was more like a minute, thought Nick.

"Yes!" said Cyclone Maylor, putting up his hand.

"Yes!" said Jerry Wong. In the next instant every guy there said "Yes" and had his hand in the air.

Mom's face lit up. "Thanks, boys," she said. "From now on you can call me Coach."

Mom wrote the names of each player down on a tablet she had brought with her. After their names she wrote their positions. Then she asked one of the players

16

to hit fly balls to the outfielders and another player to hit to the infielders. There were fourteen players altogether, including two pitchers, Johnny Linn and Frankie Morrow. She had them shag fly balls, too.

Cyclone Maylor and Bill Dakes alternated at second base. Cyclone was hustling and yelling every minute. Bill wasn't. Nick, watching from deep short, felt that Bill wasn't doing his best. Bill hardly made an effort for a ground ball that sizzled past him to the outfield.

"Come on, Bill!" yelled Mom. "Shake a leg out there!"

Bill moved faster after the next one.

Someone laughed nearby. A deepthroated, amused laugh. Nick saw a car parked on the roadside with a man behind the wheel. The car started up and sped down the road.

"Who was that?" asked Mom, curious.

"Burt Stevens," said Russ Gray, the first baseman. "He coaches the Tornadoes, the team that won the pennant the last two years."

"Is that so?" A peculiar light glimmered in Mom's eyes. "Well, maybe by the end of this season he'll laugh out of the other side of his mouth."

A week later Mom made a phone call and scheduled a practice game with — of all teams, thought Nick — the Tornadoes. The game was at six-thirty, Friday.

The Vasseys ate supper early that day. Nick had just finished eating when the Matsons' car pulled up in front of the house. Mrs. Matson was driving and had Gale, Dave and Marge with her.

"Mom, I'm going over to Gale's house

18

for a while," said Nick. "He wants to show me his aquarium."

"Okay," said Mom. "But don't be late for the game."

Gale lived near the edge of Flat Rock. His father, the only black on the police force, used to play professional baseball. He would make a good coach, thought Nick. Too bad he had to work evenings.

The fifteen-gallon aquarium had tropical fish in it — angel fish, black mollies, zebras, neon tetras. Gale pointed the different kinds out with pride while the fish scooted about in all directions.

"Those zebras are devils," he said. "They're always chasing the other fish."

Later they went outdoors. Dave and Marge were skateboarding on the large blacktop driveway in front of the garage. Dave let Nick use his skateboard awhile,

19

and Nick had so much fun he practically forgot about baseball until Mrs. Matson stepped out on the front porch.

"You'd better hurry to your baseball game, boys," she reminded them. "It's almost six-thirty."

"Wow!" cried Nick. "Let's go, Gale! Thanks for letting me skateboard, Dave!"

He and Gale picked up their gloves and hurried to the street. Taking a shortcut through a strawberry field, they arrived at the ball park just as the Thunderball infielders were running out to take their practice.

Jim Rennie was running out to shortstop, Nick's usual position. Nick wondered if Mom was going to let Jim play shortstop even though he, Nick, had gotten to the game in time.

When Nick and Gale ran up, puffing, in

front of the dugout, Mom was handing a ball to Johnny Linn to hit to the infielders. Near first base, Bill Dakes, a utility infielder, was hitting flies to the outfielders.

"Well," Mom said a bit firmly, "I wondered whether you boys had decided to play baseball or go fishing. Nick, work out there with Jim. Gale, trot to the outfield and shag flies with those other boys."

"I'm sorry, Mrs. Vassey," Gale started to apologize. "It was my fault that we —"

"Never mind," Mom interrupted. "Get going. We don't have much time."

Johnny's hits to the infielders were soft and easy to handle. They were nothing like the hard grounders Dad used to hit to them. As far as Nick was concerned, the practice meant nothing more than a little exercise.

Then it was time for the Tornadoes to

take their turn on the field. While they did so Mom reshuffled the lineup slightly.

It was as follows when she was done:

Cyclone Maylor	2b
Jerry Wong	cf
Nick Vassey	ss
Gale Matson	lf
Russ Gray	1b
Wayne Snow	c
Scotty Page	rf
Jim Rennie	3b
Frankie Morrow	p

An umpire of the regular season had accepted the job of umpiring this non-league game. Nick picked up a bat and crouched on one knee in front of the dugout. Waiting for the first pitch from the Tornadoes' tall left-hander, Lefty Burns, was Cyclone Maylor.

Lefty breezed the first pitch by Cyclone for a called strike, then slipped another one by him. Cyclone yanked nervously on his helmet while Mom yelled to him to "swing when it's in there!"

Crack! A high soaring fly to center. The Tornadoes' center fielder moved forward three steps and caught it easily. Jerry Wong socked a grass-cutting grounder down to third for out number two, and Nick was up.

"Here he is!" shouted Bugs Wheeler, the Tornadoes' catcher. "The big one, Lefty!"

And to Nick: "What's your mother been doing, Nick? Taking coaching lessons? Ha!"

Nick glared at Bugs and set his teeth. He watched the first pitch come in, but he was too rattled to be ready for it.

"Strike!" said the ump.

Bugs laughed again. " 'Ataway to go, Lefty! Pitch to me, baby! I think I got his number!"

3

NICK braced himself for the next pitch. He tried to forget Bugs's remark, but you can't forget remarks like that very easily.

The pitch. "Ball!"

The next was in there and Nick swung. Crack! A sharp line drive over third! Nick dropped his bat and started to bolt to first base. But he saw the ball curve and strike the ground just inches outside the foul line and he stopped.

"Tough luck, Nick!" shouted Mom.

Bugs was grinning when Nick picked

24

up the bat to try again. "Too bad, Nick. Maybe your coach could tell you what you did wrong that time."

Shut up! Nick wanted to say. But that would only make Bugs's remarks worse than ever.

"Ball two!"

Lefty couldn't get the next two pitches over either, and Nick walked. He flashed a quick grin at Bugs as he tossed the bat aside. But Bugs wasn't looking at him now.

Gale Matson fouled the first pitch, then drove a sky-rocketing fly to short center field. The shortstop, second baseman and center fielder all ran after it. It was the center fielder who yelled for it and caught it. Three outs.

A pop fly to Nick, a grounder to Jim, and a caught foul tip on the third strike ended the half-inning for the Tornadoes. In the top of the second the Thunderballs picked up their first run, but the Tornadoes put across three on a home run by Bugs with two on. Bugs Wheeler. The guy Nick least wanted to see crack out a homer.

In the top of the third, with one out, Cyclone scored from second on Nick's double. Gale singled, a worm-wiggling grounder that just got by Lefty Burns. Russ Gray walked, filling the bases. Then Wayne Snow hit into a double play, leaving two stranded.

The Tornadoes started to hit Frankie hard in the bottom of the third. They scored a run and still had three men on. Nick looked at Mom sitting in the dugout and wondered why she let Frankie continue pitching. It just proved that she didn't know enough about baseball.

Another run scored and Nick wished now that the Thunderballs had not voted Mom in to coach. She just didn't know what to do at the crucial times, that's all there was to it.

Somehow the Thunderballs got the third out and went to bat, hoping to start a rally of their own. They couldn't. The Tornadoes came back up in the last of the fourth and started where they had left off in the third inning. They were knocking Frankie's pitches all over the lot, and Nick wished he and Gale had stayed away entirely. Mom just was no coach.

And then, after three runs scored and only one out, Mom decided to do something. "Time!" she yelled, running out of the dugout and waving her arms at the umpire. "Johnny! Johnny Linn! Come on!"

"Now we're going to see some strategy!" yelled Bugs Wheeler from the Tornadoes' dugout.

Johnny Linn trotted in from the bullpen where he had been warming up, took the ball from Frankie and stepped onto the mound. He threw a few pitches to Wayne Snow, then stepped off the rubber. The umpire called, "Play ball," and the game resumed.

Nick saw Burt Stevens sitting in the Tornadoes' dugout with a Cheshire-cat grin on his face. Matter of fact, the whole team seemed to be grinning like that. He just could not understand why Mom got a practice game with them when there were weaker teams in the league. She just could not have been thinking.

Johnny Linn got the next two men out without letting the Tornadoes score. But the Tornadoes picked up three more runs during the next two innings to the Thunderballs' two and won the game 11 to 4.

"Better luck next time, Coach!" Coach Stevens yelled over at Mom, the cat grin on his face.

Mom smiled back. "We're not worrying, Mr. Stevens! The real fight has not yet begun!"

Nick stared at her. *What* was she saying? Wasn't it enough that she was a woman without saying a thing like that?

The next day Jerry Wong came over with Scotty and took turns playing chess with Nick. Jerry's father ran the only Chinese-American restaurant in Flat Rock.

Next to baseball, Nick liked chess best.

Matter of fact, now that Mom was coaching he probably liked chess better.

Nick won once, Scotty once, and Jerry twice. In both of Jerry's games his queen and rook tied up his opponent's king so quickly that the guys hardly knew what had happened.

After their chess games the next day, they went outdoors to skateboard. Most of the kids in the neighborhood skateboarded at one time or another on the sidewalks. Even Jen and Sue had skateboards of their own.

"Nick, look!"

Nick swung around at Jen's voice, almost losing his balance and falling off the skateboard. There was Jerry Wong on his skateboard, standing on his hands. The guys and girls looked at him as if transfixed.

"Hey!" Nick said. "You practicing for some show or something?"

Jerry grinned at him. "No. I just learned this yesterday."

A chess hotshot, now a skateboard hotshot, thought Nick. What was the guy going to do next?

"Hah!" smirked Scotty. "He's just showing off for the girls."

That did it. Jerry got off the board and on it with his feet.

"You lunkhead," snapped Jen. "You embarrassed him."

"I didn't mean to," apologized Scotty.

Jerry was smiling, however, his face red from having stood on his hands. It was hard to tell whether he was embarrassed or not. But he wasn't sore. That was the important thing. He was sensitive, but seldom had Nick seen him sore.

The boys rode down the sidewalk and started to turn past the corner drugstore when something in the field across Columbus Street caught their attention. A boy was riding a shiny black horse, sitting straight on its bare back while it trotted as hard as it probably could. The boy was Wayne Snow. He looked at the guys for an instant, and then looked away.

Scotty sighed. "Well, la de da!" he sang. "Isn't it nice to be rich? You can pretend you don't know the guys you play baseball with."

Down the highway a bit was a big white house where Wayne lived with his parents. When they were home, that is. Otherwise there was no one except him, his older brother Ron, and a housekeeper. Mrs. Snow was always traipsing about the country putting on fashion shows, and Mr.

Snow was usually away on a business trip. Nick didn't know exactly what he did.

Just then two kids on skateboards rounded the corner a block away and started up the sidewalk toward the boys.

"Hey, look who's there!" one of them shouted. "Nick, I heard your Mom's coaching the Thunderballs!"

Jabber Kane was one kid with the perfect nickname.

"So what?" said Nick. The kid with Jabber was Steve Dale. Both boys played with the Clowns.

Jabber laughed as they approached. "Who ever heard of a woman coaching a boys' baseball team?"

"What difference does it make?" snapped Nick. "She probably knows more about baseball than your whole bunch of Clowns put together."

Jabber's wide smile showed large teeth

34

in front, teeth that Nick felt like knocking down Jabber's skinny throat.

"I can't wait till we play you guys," said Jabber. "I can picture your Mom yelling from the dugout, 'Come on, boys! Don't slide unless you have to! You mustn't get your pants dirty!' Ha!"

The guys laughed. Including Scotty and Jerry. Nick saw red. He squared his jaw and went after Jabber, his fists clenched. Jabber whisked around on his skateboard and sped off down the sidewalk, his laughter trailing after him.

"Forget it," said Scotty. "He's only kidding."

"I know," replied Nick. "But I don't like it. I hope that when we play those Clowns we'll beat them twenty to nothing."

What he really wished, though, was that someone else were coaching the Thunderballs. Someone else, not Mom.

4

"MAKE a lot of noise out there," Mom told the boys. "Let Johnny know he has nothing to worry about."

With that final order from the coach, the Thunderballs ran out on the field. It was July 5, the Thunderballs' first game of the season. At bat were the Knicks, a scrappy bunch of guys who were talking it up loudly in and around their dugout as if they had the game sewn up already.

Johnny Linn, on the mound for the Thunderballs, threw in several warm-up pitches to Wayne. The umpire yelled

"Play ball!" and the Knicks' first hitter stepped to the plate. He was short and his suit was almost too big for him.

"Ball!" cried the ump, as Johnny's first pitch zipped high over the plate.

The infield chatter grew louder but it didn't help Johnny's control. He walked the batter. The next man bunted down to first. Johnny threw him out but the other runner was safe on second.

The next man lined a single over short, scoring the runner.

"Just lucky, Johnny," Nick said. He caught the throw-in from left fielder Gale Matson and tossed it to Johnny. "Let's go for two."

The Knicks' batter socked a bouncing grounder to short. Nick caught it and whipped it to second. Cyclone caught it, snapped it to first. A double play!

37

"There you go!" smiled Nick.

"You asked for it," Johnny smiled back at him.

"Cyclone Maylor! Jerry Wong! Nick Vassey!" Mom read off the names of the first three hitters. "Let's get that run back!"

Cyclone let two strikes go past him, then socked a cloud-high drive above the pitcher's mound. The Knicks' third baseman took it for the first out. Jerry let a strike go by, then took four straight balls for a free pass to first. Nick came up, looked over a couple, then hit a slow grounder to third. The third baseman fielded it, looked toward second, saw that he couldn't get Jerry, and threw to first. Out.

Gale pounded a long fly to center. Three away.

The Knicks came up, eager to pile up runs. But they didn't get any. Instead it was the Thunderballs who began popping the ball in between the Knicks. Russell Gray started it off with a single, followed by Wayne Snow's hot grounder over the third-base bag. Scotty Page drove a long fly to right which was caught, but which advanced Russ to third.

"Only one out!" yelled Mom, standing in front of the dugout with a finger jabbing the air. "Play it safe!"

"Thataway to talk to 'em, Coach!" a fan yelled from the stands. Other fans made remarks, too. They were sure getting a big kick out of seeing a woman coach a baseball team.

The remarks embarrassed Nick as he stood in the third-base coaching box. The people were having a good time, all right. But it was mostly over watching and listening to Mom. The game had little to do with it. That was how it seemed anyway.

Pat Krupa singled, driving in Russ. Wayne advanced all around to third. Then Johnny Linn singled to left, scoring Wayne. The fans stood up and clapped their hands thunderously, particularly the young fans. Jen and Sue were with a bunch of girls and they were shouting louder than ever.

The lead-off man, Cyclone, was up again. Monk Jones, the Knicks' tall right-hander, breezed a third strike by him for the Thunderballs' second out. Then Jerry popped up to the catcher, ending the rally and the bottom of the second inning.

Mom patted Johnny's back as he started out of the dugout. "Keep your pitches in there, Johnny," she said. "You've got good boys behind you."

Johnny simply nodded. He was a quiet kid. A half-dozen words from him equaled a thousand from Cyclone.

The Knicks started to hit. A double over second base. A single between third and short. A long fly to second which Jerry caught, but which accounted for a run after the runner tagged up. Two more runs scored before the Thunderballs could settle down and make the second and third outs.

Knicks 4 — Thunderballs 2.

It was the Knicks fans' turn to yell now. "How do you like them apples, Coach Vassey?" one of them said.

"That's right," Wayne said softly. "That's just the beginning."

Nick stared at him. "That's a fine thing to say, Wayne."

Mom, standing nearby, smiled. "That's being a defeatist, Wayne. We won't win if you feel that way."

Wayne's face turned beet red.

5

NICK led off in the bottom of the third.

"A home run, Nick!" Jen yelled in that soprano voice of hers. "Over the fence!"

Monk Jones rubbed the ball, nodded with satisfaction at the signal from his catcher, then stretched and delivered. Nick pulled back his bat, saw that the pitch was going wide and held his swing.

"Ball!" yelled the ump.

Monk drilled the next pitch across the inside corner for a strike. Nick cut at the next one and heard the ball plop into the catcher's mitt.

"He's your man, Monk, ol' boy!" shouted the Knicks' catcher.

Nick stepped out of the box, rubbed the bat gingerly, and looked at Monk. Monk might try to fool him with a curve this time. He stepped back into the box.

The pitch came in close, then curved away. Nick swung. *Crack!* The ball struck the ground in front of Monk, bounced high over his head and then over second base for a single. The fans yelled as Nick stood on the bag at first and looked at Mom for a bunt signal. But she gave none.

Gale, up next, blasted the first pitch in a line drive over second. Nick swept around second base and headed for third.

"Go! Go! Go!" third-base coach Tom

Warren shouted, swinging his left arm like a windmill.

Nick rounded third and raced for home. As he got close to it he heard Mom and some of the guys yelling to him, "Hit it, Nick! Hit the dirt!"

Nick did. The catcher caught the relay and put it on Nick, but Nick was already across the plate. "Safe!" cried the ump.

Nick got up, brushed off his pants and saw Gale trotting back to second base for a clean double. "Nice running, Nick," Mom said. "Okay, Russ! Let's keep it going!"

Russell Gray fouled the first two pitches to the backstop screen, let an inside pitch go by, then went down swinging. Next batter was Wayne Snow. He walked to the plate, dragging his bat over the ground.

"Look at him," muttered Scotty disgust-

edly. "How are we going to win with him acting like that?"

"Liven up, Wayne!" snapped Cyclone. "This is a ball game, not a funeral!"

"All right, all right," cautioned Mom. "Cut out the remarks."

Wayne swung at a high pitch and drove it in a line over the fence. It went foul. He

swung at the next pitch and sent it a mile
into the sky. This one dropped behind the
home-plate stands.

"Straighten it out, Wayne!" Mom
shouted.

There was a chuckle in the stands and
Nick looked over at Mom. Either she had
not heard it or she wasn't letting on she

had. Her shout did sound funny, though, coming from the dugout. After thinking about it, he felt a funny sensation — a sensation of pride. It took a lot of nerve to do what Mom was doing.

Monk's next three pitches were balls. Then Wayne stepped into a sidearm pitch, swung hard, and missed completely. He walked back to the dugout, dragging the bat, not looking anywhere except at the ground.

"Forget it, Wayne," said Mom. "You'll be up again."

Scotty waited out Monk's pitches and got a free ticket to first. Pat came up, took two balls and a strike, then laced a drive to deep center field. It sure looked as if it were heading for the Great Beyond. But the Knicks' center fielder, running back as hard as he could, reached up his gloved hand and nabbed it.

The Knicks came up and put across two more runs to give them a 6 to 3 lead. With two on and two out the Knicks' batter drove a hot liner directly at Nick. It was high. Nick leaped, stretching as far as he could. *Pop!* He had it!

He ran in from short, sweat dripping off his face. A few inches higher and that ball would have gone over his head and two more runs would have scored.

He looked sorrowfully at Mom. Her first game, he thought, and they were going to lose it. She caught his eye and smiled.

I don't know, he thought. We're losing the game and she looks as happy as if we were winning it. If Dad were in her place, *he* wouldn't be smiling. You could bet your life on that.

49

6

JOHNNY LINN led off in the bottom of the fourth inning with a colossal triple to left center field. It sure looked like a good start. But Bill Dakes, batting for Cyclone, grounded out to third and Jerry Wong bounced one back to the pitcher for the second out.

"Oh, no!" Mom moaned. "Jim, bat for Nick! Wait for a good one! Tom, get ready to bat for Gale."

Nick tossed his bat onto the pile fanned out on the ground and returned to the dugout. He wasn't happy about being replaced, but he knew that Mom wanted every player on the team to play at least three innings. It was a league rule that every player had to play at least two innings. Mom preferred to be a little more generous whenever she could.

Jim Rennie drew a walk. Then Tom Warren walked, filling the bases!

The Thunderballs' dugout livened up like a beehive. "A grand slammer, Russ!" yelled Nick. "Clean the bases!"

Russ wiggled the toes of his sneakers into the soft, dusty earth, tugged at his protective helmet, then got ready for Monk's pitch. The ball came in slightly high. Russ swung, and missed.

"Too high, Russ!" Cyclone shouted.

The next was high, too. Again he swung and missed. The Thunderball fans groaned. Monk pitched another high one. This one Russ let go by. Ball one.

Monk threw two more balls for a three-two count, then rifled the next one in knee-high. Russ swung hard and missed for strike three. Three away. Russ tossed his bat angrily toward the dugout and ran out to his position at first base. Nick knew exactly how he felt. He had struck out with the bases loaded a few times himself.

"Scotty," said Mom, as Scotty started out of the dugout, "wait. Mike, take right field."

"Yes, sir," said Mike Todey. "I mean, yes, ma'am."

Nick grinned. Guess it was going to be a long while before most of the boys would be calling Mom "Coach."

The Knicks picked up a run in the top of the fifth with a double and then an error by Jim Rennie. He had made a neat catch on a fast bouncing ball, but pegged it too high to first base. The runner on second scored on the overthrow. The run was the only one the Knicks got.

The Thunderballs started off like a straw fire during their turn at bat. Wayne Snow belted a hot grounder that zipped over the third-base bag for a double. Mike Todey singled him in and Pat Krupa drew a pass.

"Look at Pat," said Scotty. "He wobbles like a duck. I can't see how he can run as fast as he does."

"He pulls back all levers and goes when he has to," Nick said, grinning.

Johnny Linn, up next, also drew a walk, filling the bases. Again the Thunderballs' fans grew excited and began to yell for a hit. Any kind of hit.

Bill Dakes tapped the tip of his bat against the plate, lifted it to his shoulder, and waited for the pitch. It was high. Ball one. He swung at the next pitch and laced it to left field. The fielder hardly had to move. Mike Todey, on third, stayed on the bag until the ball was caught, then bolted for home. He made it easily.

Jerry Wong took a called strike, then belted a searing grounder directly at the shortstop. The guy fielded it, snapped it to second. Second to first. A double play. Three outs.

"We picked up two, anyway," said Mom. "Now get out there and hold them."

Hold them they did. Johnny struck out the first man and the next two grounded out. The Thunderballs came up for the last time. They were trailing 7 to 5. Fat chance they had of winning this ball game thought Nick. It would have been a good start to have won the first league game for Mom.

Jim Rennie led off and smashed the second pitch for a clean single over second. Then Tom Warren popped out to put a damper on the Thunderballs' hopes of getting a run. Russ, having struck out the last two times at bat, didn't raise anyone's hopes as he strode to the plate. He took a called strike, a ball, then hammered a solid drive to right center field! Jim raced all around to home and Russ took second on the play on Jim.

Wayne went down swinging. Two away. And two runs from winning the ball game. It still seemed hopeless.

Then Mike walked. Pat hit a grounder to short. It was fumbled! Russ held up at third, Mike at second. Pat was on first. The tying run — and the winning run — were on base!

"Win your own ball game, Johnny!"

yelled a fan. "Chase home those ducks!"

Johnny Linn waited out the pitches. Then, with the count two and two, he swung at a chest-high pitch. *Crack!* A line drive over the shortstop's head! Russ scored. Mike scored. Pat halted on third, leaving Johnny with a double.

The game was over. The Thunderballs were the winners, 8 to 7. Mom had won her first league ball game.

7

TWO days later the Thunderballs tangled with the Zebras. Mom had Bill Dakes and Jim Rennie start in place of Cyclone and Nick. The Thunderballs had first raps, but in the first two innings they could do little against their opponents. Eddie Cash, the Zebras' little right-hander, didn't seem to have much on the ball, yet no Thunderball could hit him.

Frankie Morrow, pitching for the Thunderballs, was tagged for four hits and three runs in the two innings. He led off the third with a single, though, and Bill sacri-

ficed him to second on a bunt. Then Jerry
Wong tripled, scoring Frankie, and Jim
hit a high fly which landed between three
fielders for a freak double, scoring Jerry.
It was funny the way the three Zebras
stood there, each expecting the other to
catch the ball.

"Remember that incident," Mom said.
"If that ever happens to you, *someone call
for the ball.* Don't let it drop between
you."

The two runs were all the Thunderballs
scored that half-inning. In the top of the
fourth Mike Todey, batting for Scotty
Page, walked. Then Gale, pinch-hitting for
Pat Krupa, walloped a home run over the
left-field fence. Two singles and an error
accounted for another run and the Thunderballs went into the lead, 5 to 3.

Nick smiled as he trotted out to short,

replacing Jim Rennie. It looked as if Mom's Thunderballs were heading for their second straight victory.

The Zebras squeezed in a run in the bottom of the fourth, but the Thunderballs got it back in the fifth. And then, in the bottom of the fifth, the Zebras pulled out all stops and really poured it on the Thunderballs. They collected five hits and four runs for a total of eight runs. The Thunderballs drew a goose egg in the sixth and that was it. The Zebras won 8 to 6.

"Well," Mom said, heaving a sigh, "we can't win them all."

"We were just lucky to win the first one," muttered Wayne Snow.

Mom stared at him. "Lucky, did you say?"

Wayne's face turned cherry red. "Well, maybe we weren't."

He climbed out of the dugout, picked up the catcher's mitt and shoved it inside the canvas bag where the other baseball equipment was kept. Then he hung around, cleaning his fingernails, while the color of his face gradually returned to normal.

Mom looked at Wayne as if trying to figure him out. She told the boys to put the bats and balls into the bag and then put the bag into her car.

"Come on, Wayne," Mom said, when they were ready to leave. "You can ride with us as far as our house."

He seemed reluctant at first. Then he shrugged and got into the car. Nick thought that Mom would say something more to Wayne, but she didn't. And he was glad. Wayne looked as if he didn't care to talk about anything.

Wayne helped Nick lift the equipment

out of the car when they reached home. Wayne spotted the tent Dad had put in the yard for Nick. "That's a beauty. Ever spend a night in it?"

"Oh, sure," said Nick. He met Wayne's eyes. "Wayne, you're not very happy about my mother's coaching us, are you?"

Wayne's lips twitched. "I didn't say anything."

"No. But that's what you're thinking, isn't it? I'm not too keen about it, either. And some of the other guys feel the same way. But nobody else will coach us. If she didn't coach us we wouldn't have a team. Did you ask your Dad if he'd like to coach us?"

Wayne didn't answer for a while. At last he said, "Your mother's okay. I'm just not crazy about baseball. I've even thought of quitting. I don't know. Maybe I will or maybe I won't."

He walked away. When he was halfway to the sidewalk he turned and said over his shoulder, "So long. And thanks for the ride."

Nick frowned after him. Wayne quitting? Did he really mean it? He really was a strange kid. Why hadn't he answered those questions about his father? What did his father do that made him unable to coach the team? Was it because he didn't know enough about baseball? Or was it some other reason?

Nick went into the house and saw that Dad was home. He certainly was putting in some long hours lately.

"Dad, do you know Mr. Snow? Know what his job is?"

Dad shrugged. "He's an importer, I think. Brings goods in from abroad. Why?"

"Wayne never talks about him."

"Maybe Wayne doesn't know exactly what he does," answered Dad.

It sure seemed funny. *He* knew what *his* dad did.

On Saturday afternoon Gale and Scotty came over and the three of them rode their skateboards down to the corner. They stopped in the drugstore for ice-cream cones and rode on the sidewalk on Columbus Street till they were opposite Wayne Snow's house.

Nick heard sharp, cracking sounds coming from the place, and saw baseballs flying through the air on the other side of the garage.

"How do you like that?" he said. "He's practicing batting! And the other day he said he didn't like baseball!"

8

THE boys picked up their skateboards and walked over to the other side of the garage.

Johnny Linn, with a half a dozen baseballs at his feet, was pitching them in to Wayne who was standing with his back to the garage.

"Hi!" greeted Nick. "Getting in some practice?"

"Hi," said Johnny.

"Hi," said Wayne, and shrugged. "I need it, don't I?"

"Thought you said you might quit baseball," said Nick. "You wouldn't do this if you were going to quit, would you?"

Wayne shrugged. "I said it because I can't hit. Then Johnny said he was willing to pitch to me."

"He said I could ride his horse," Johnny said.

"Let's quit." Wayne tossed his bat to the ground. "I've had enough, anyway."

Nick noticed a swimming pool to the left of the garage, encircled by a high wire fence. There was a small, child-size rowboat in the pool with oars inside it. There were several canvas lounging chairs and a sun umbrella, folded down over a table, along the side of the pool.

This Wayne kid has everything, thought Nick. And what he didn't have, he probably could get. All he had to do was ask for it. What a life!

A car turned into the driveway. A long black sports car so clean and shiny you could see your reflection in it. It stopped and a young man in slacks and a sporty sweater hopped out of it.

"Hi, gang," he greeted cheerfully, and looked at Wayne. "Sorry to bust up your

fun, brother, but we're driving up to the cottage."

Wayne frowned. "Now?"

"Now. Get Mrs. Lane to pack your clothes. Make sure there's enough for two weeks."

"*Two weeks?*"

"Two weeks," repeated his big brother. "Come on. Let's go." He bounded to the house in his white sneakers. Probably, thought Nick, they had a tennis court next to their cottage. And if the cottage was beside a lake they probably had a boat, too.

"Your mother and father, are they at the cottage?" Nick asked.

"Just my mother," replied Wayne. "She went there —" he faltered and swallowed. "Well, she's been away a couple of days on that business she's got with dresses and stuff and went to the cottage when she got through. Dad's going there later."

He didn't seem impressed about going at all.

"Wayne!" shouted his brother from the side porch of the house. "Are you coming or aren't you?"

"I'm coming," said Wayne, not enthusiastically. "Nick, will you tell your mother that I won't be at the games for the next couple of weeks? I hope she won't have trouble getting somebody to catch."

"I'll tell her," said Nick.

Suddenly he thought: Who else *could* catch for the Thunderballs? Boy! Mom's headaches in coaching a Little League baseball team were just beginning!

9

"I THINK you're the man to do it," Mom announced after she and Nick had talked about the catching position for a while. "You're strong and you have a good arm. A good arm's a major ingredient for a catcher, isn't it?"

"Yes, but I've never caught before, Mom. I don't know anything about signals."

"One finger's for a straight ball, two fingers for a hook," explained Mom. "You don't have to worry about that anyway.

70

Johnny will be pitching against the Tornadoes. He knows the batters pretty well. If he doesn't like what you're calling for he'll shake it off."

She smiled as she said it, as if Johnny Linn were a big-leaguer or something. He didn't say any more. Fact was, he could not think of anyone else on the team who had caught before either. And Wayne was going to be gone for two weeks. That meant that Nick would have to catch about four games.

Jim Rennie, who was going to play shortstop, was a weak infielder, too. So there were two positions which had been weakened because of Wayne's not playing. Nick shook his head sadly. He could see the Thunderballs coming out on the tail end of the next three or four games.

Poor Mom! She probably will wish she

had not volunteered to take on a coaching job.

Burt Stevens, the Tornadoes' coach, hit hard grounders to his infielders and kept them hustling every minute. Nick knew what he must be thinking. Mr. Stevens had won the pennant the last two years and he wasn't going to let a woman coach stop him from winning it again this year.

The Tornadoes, batting first, got on to Johnny's pitching almost immediately. They chalked up two runs before the Thunderballs could get them out.

"That's the way we'll be getting them!" Bugs Wheeler yelled loud enough for everybody to hear. "Two runs at a time!"

Nick felt his neck burn. How he hoped he could make Bugs eat those words!

Bill Dakes walked and Jerry Wong singled to get them off to a good start. But Nick hit into a double play, and Tom Warren flied out to left, ending the half-inning without a run.

In the top of the second the Tornadoes didn't score either.

"Where are those two runs, Bugs?" Nick yelled across the diamond.

"We'll make it up the next time!" Bugs yelled back.

The Thunderballs picked up one run on Mike's single and a triple by Pat Krupa. The Tornadoes came back with a run in the top of the third. But it was only one run, not two. And then there was a shout from one of the guys and Nick saw Wayne Snow come trotting around the corner of the dugout.

"Wayne!" he shouted, followed by a

73

similar chorus from the other guys. "Am I glad to see you!"

Wayne was in uniform, ready to play. His face beamed. "My brother drove me down," he explained. "He's going to do it every time we have a game. He doesn't mind. It's only sixty miles to our cottage."

Only sixty miles, thought Nick. Ron probably covered it in no time in that sports car of his.

"I'm glad to see you, too, Wayne," said Mom. "When this half-inning's over, take over the catching job from Nick. I'm sure he won't mind." She looked from Nick to Jim, as if trying to decide which to let play shortstop. Then she said, "Jim, let Nick take over short, will you?"

"Sure, Coach," Jim said.

Nick knew that making a decision between him and Jim was tough. Mom didn't want anyone to feel that she was favoring him. But in this game, it seemed best that he play.

Bill Dakes led off with a single over second and Jerry advanced him to third on a double to left center field. It seemed that their hitting streak ended right there, for Nick grounded out to first and Tom Warren fanned. Then Russ walked, loading the bases.

"You want Wayne to bat for me?" Jim asked Mom. He had his helmet on, ready to go to the plate.

"With the bases filled?" Mom smiled. "No, Jim. You get up there and hit the ball. Drive in those runs."

Jim walked to the plate, settled his helmet better on his head, and waited for the pitch from Bob Kreel, the Tornadoes' tall right-hander.

"Strike one!" yelled the ump as Bob breezed the ball past Jim.

The next was a ball. So was the next. Then Jim tagged one. A long high fly toward the left-field fence. The Tornadoes' outfielder ran back after it but it was no use. It went over the fence for a grand-slam homer.

Everyone, including Mom, stepped out of the dugout and shook Jim's hand as he trotted in. And the Thunderballs' fans yelled as they had never yelled before. Mike flied out, ending the rally. Tornadoes 3 — Thunderballs 5.

Then the Tornadoes started rolling. They didn't stop until they had collected three runs, surging ahead of the Thunderballs 6 to 5.

"Hey, Thunderballs! We're just kidding with you!" yelled a Tornado sitting on the bench. "Watch what happens the next two innings!"

"You watch, too!" snorted Gale. "Because you're not going to do anything!"

Mom smiled at him. "Thataway, Gale. Let's show them that *we're* not kidding."

10

CYCLONE batted for Pat in the bottom of the fourth and slammed a two-one pitch to deep center. It looked good until the center fielder reached up his gloved hand and pulled it out of the air.

Johnny Linn grounded out on the first pitch and Bill Dakes flied out to right. It was a fast half-inning.

The Tornadoes connected with two clean hits through the infield. Then Nick made a nice stop at short and threw the ball to Bill to start a double play. Too wide! One run scored! Scotty Page, who had taken Mike's place in right field, retrieved the ball and pegged it in.

Nick tightened his lips with disgust. He had been too hasty and not careful. There were still two men on — one on first, the other on third. "C'mon, Johnny! C'mon, kid! They won't do it again, Johnny!"

A long fly to deep center. Jerry Wong caught it, pegged it in. Bill caught the peg and relayed it home, but not in time. The runner had tagged up at third and scored. Johnny fanned the next two batters to retire the side. But the Tornadoes had chalked up two runs to boost their total to 8.

Jerry, leading off in the bottom of the fifth, received a nice ovation as he strode to the plate. That was a good catch he had made in center field. He took a called strike, a ball, then belted a hard grounder through the pitcher's box for a single. Nick, up next, socked a hard grounder to second. The second baseman fumbled it and Nick was safe at first, Jerry safe at second.

Gale, batting for Tom Warren, blasted a double between left and center, scoring Jerry. But the fielder retrieved the ball quickly and the coach held Nick up at third.

No outs so far. Nick wished that somebody would hit him in. But Russ struck out, Wayne popped to short, and Scotty flied to left. Dismally Nick shook his head, picked up his glove and ran out to his position.

In the top of the sixth the Tornadoes picked up another run to help make their lead more secure — 9 to 6. It was the Thunderballs' last chance at bat. Their last chance to overtake the Tornadoes.

The Thunderballs' bench was silent as

Cyclone put on his helmet, picked up his bat and went to the plate.

"What is this?" said Mom. "A funeral wake? Let's hear some chatter. Come on. Liven up!"

Across the way, on the Tornadoes' bench, Nick saw a smug look on Coach Stevens's face, as if the coach was having the time of his life. If only the Thunderballs could do something to wipe that smile off, thought Nick. If only *he* could do something. But he was fifth to bat and might not get his chance.

The first pitch to Cyclone. He swung. A single over short! Then Johnny belted a low pitch that glanced off the pitcher's left foot and sailed through the space between first and second. Bill Dakes hit a grounder to the shortstop's right side. The shortstop fielded it and threw to second, getting out Johnny. The second baseman pegged to first to try for a double play, but Bill Dakes beat the throw by a step. One away, runners on first and third.

The Thunderballs' fans were roaring now. "Keep it up, Jerry!" one of them yelled. "Let's turn this game upside down!"

Nick, on one knee in front of the dugout, hoped Jerry would get a hit. A double play would end the game, and Nick wanted so much to bat again and have a chance to wipe that smug look off Coach Stevens's face.

Bob Kreel stretched, delivered. Ball one. The next was a strike. Then Jerry swung at a high one and popped it up. Two outs. Winning sure looked impossible.

"Tag it, Nick," said Gale. "Save me a rap."

Nick tugged at his helmet and stepped to the plate. Bob Kreel stretched, pitched. "Strike!" yelled the ump.

Then, "Strike two!" Nick stepped out of the box and glanced at the umpire. He didn't like that call but he said nothing.

"Ball!"

One and two was the count. The next pitch came in and Nick swung. *Crack!* A long, high fly heading for the left-field fence! The fielder ran back . . . back . . . Over the fence it went! A home run!

Nick circled the bases, a grin on his face as he crossed the plate. The whole gang, including Mom, stood outside the dugout and shook his hand.

"It's all tied up!" Mom exclaimed. "One more run to go!"

"There you are, Gale!" smiled Nick.

Gale grinned. "Thanks, Nick." He took

a called strike, then smashed a searing double to left field!

Russ Gray was next up to bat.

"Drive him in, Russ!" yelled Mom. "A single will do it!"

Bob Kreel took his time. He threw nothing good in his first three pitches. Then he poured in a strike, then another for a three-two count. His next was good, too. Russ belted it. A clean single over short! Gale scored and the game was over. Thunderballs 10 — Tornadoes 9.

Coach Stevens came over and shook Mom's hand. "Congratulations, Coach," he said, smiling broadly. "You came through like a veteran."

Mom smiled pleasantly. "Thank you, Coach. Maybe we were a little . . . lucky?"

Nick felt that Mom was really enjoying

the moment, paying back Coach Stevens a little of the needling he and his team had been giving her and the Thunderballs.

Coach Stevens cleared his throat. "Well, I can't say that. Your boys were hitting very well toward the end. But don't worry," he added, chuckling, "you don't think for a minute that I'm going to let a woman beat me out of another pennant, do you?"

Mom shrugged as if the idea had not occurred to her before. "It would be something to remember, wouldn't it?" she said.

11

A THOUGHT occurred to Nick right after dinner the next day. It was a hot, sticky night. Nobody was home at the Snows. Nobody would know . . .

"Hey, guys," he said to Gale and Scotty when they came over. "Let's go swimming in Wayne Snow's swimming pool. Nobody's home there. Why let that big beautiful pool go to waste?"

"How about their housekeeper?" questioned Scotty. "Isn't she there?"

"She lives in her own home. She wouldn't be there now." The idea became better and better all the time.

"Wayne's a funny guy," Gale said doubtfully. "Think he'd get sore at us if he found out?"

"Who's going to tell him?" said Nick.

Gale and Scotty looked at each other, then both shrugged. "Guess it's all right," said Gale.

"Why not?" said Scotty. "We're not going to hurt the water, are we? Even if Wayne does find out, he wouldn't care."

"Let's go!" cried Nick, so pleased with the idea he couldn't wait to get to the pool.

Each boy picked up his swimming trunks at his house. They met at the Snows' house and changed into their trunks on the back porch. The gate was locked, so they climbed over the wire fence to the pool.

The boys dived in and swam from one end of the pool to the other. Then they ducked each other and laughed, having the time of their lives. The water was warm, perfect.

Nick didn't know how long they had been in the pool — fifteen minutes . . . maybe twenty — when he saw that Gale suddenly had stopped swimming and was looking at something, or *someone*, beyond the pool. Nick followed his friend's gaze and then froze.

A tall, lean-faced man in a light gray suit and wearing a narrow-brimmed hat stood there on the other side of the fence, looking at them. He was smiling, but his smile wasn't warm enough to ease Nick's panic. They were caught swimming in the pool, in a private pool where they had no business being. That was all Nick could think about at the moment.

"Hi," the man greeted them in a voice so polite it surprised Nick. "How's the water?"

Nick stared at Gale, then saw Scotty pop out of the water a yard or so to his left. "F-fine!" he stuttered.

He swam to the edge and climbed out. Gale and Scotty started to follow him.

"You don't have to get out," said the man. "I'm Mr. Snow. I think I've seen you boys in the neighborhood, haven't I?"

Nick forced a smile. It was possible that Mr. Snow had seen them, but this was the first time he had ever seen Mr. Snow.

"We live just a few blocks away," admitted Nick, grabbing up a towel and drying himself. *You're not supposed to be here, Mr. Snow!* he wanted to yell. *You're supposed to be going to your cottage. That's where your wife is. And Ron and Wayne.*

You're not supposed to catch us swimming in your pool!

That's what hurt him, getting caught swimming in the pool. Now he knew how terribly wrong it was. And it had seemed such a good idea.

He looked at Gale and Scotty. They were drying themselves, too. And looking ashamed.

"I — I'm sorry, Mr. Snow," said Nick. "This was my idea."

"I'm sorry, too, Mr. Snow," said Gale.

"So am I," said Scotty.

A small peal of laughter bubbled from Mr. Snow. "You've repented! That's good enough for me!" He waved to them. "Well, I'm on my way to our cottage to see the rest of my family. I wanted to stop here to drop off some of my work. So long, boys."

"So long, Mr. Snow." They said it almost together.

They were dressed by the time they heard Mr. Snow's car backing out of the driveway. "He's not a bad guy at all, is he?" said Nick, as he heard the car gun up the street.

"No, he isn't," said Gale. "And for that reason I'm sorrier for going into the pool than I would be if he was."

They climbed over the fence and started down the street.

"Race you to the corner," said Nick numbly.

He didn't feel like racing, though. He just wanted to say something to break the awful silence.

The Thunderballs beat the Clowns on Friday. Wayne's brother Ron had driven him to the game and Mom thanked them both.

Then Nick asked Wayne if his father

had told him about the swimming pool incident. "No," said Wayne, looking surprised. "What happened?"

"Nothing, except that Gale, Scotty and I went swimming in it and your dad caught us. We told him we were sorry."

Wayne smiled. "That's okay," he said. "Come over anytime."

"Not unless you're there," replied Nick, shaking his head. Under no circumstances would he ever go there again unless one of the Snows was home. Not only was it dangerous to swim in an unsupervised pool, but it was outright trespassing.

On Tuesday the Thunderballs rolled over the Knicks, knocking Monk Jones out of the box in the third inning. Mom was especially pleased about that.

On Thursday something unusual took place just before the game with the Zebras.

A photographer from the local paper, the Flat Rock *Sentinel,* arrived. With him was a reporter who asked Mom all sorts of questions about herself, her family, when her interest in baseball had begun and so on. The photographer took pictures of her and stayed for the game.

The Thunderballs scored twice in the third, twice in the fourth, and once in the sixth. The Zebras piled up only three runs altogether, and lost the ball game 5 to 3.

"Things weren't looking so good in the first two innings," said Cyclone as the team was loading the equipment into the car. "Those newspaper guys must have brought us good luck."

"It wasn't luck," said Mom. "You boys are getting good."

Mom, Dad, Nick and the girls went to Wong's Chinese-American Restaurant for dinner the next evening. Mr. Wong, Jerry's father, came to their table to wait on them.

"Congratulations, Mrs. Vassey," he said. "Nice picture of you in the paper. Fine write-up, too."

"Thank you, Mr. Wong," said Mom, smiling modestly.

"Well, hi, Coach," said a voice from the other side of the room. "Heard the Zebras did some sloppy playing yesterday."

All eyes turned and settled on Coach Burt Stevens sitting there with his entire family. Mrs. Stevens, the coach, and their two children began to laugh.

"Hi, Coach Stevens," greeted Mom. "Yes, we won. I thought the Thunderballs did some fine playing."

"Remember what I said before," said Coach Stevens with a chuckle. "There's still a long way to go."

Dad took a pencil and a small pad out of his pocket, wrote on the pad, tore out the sheet and folded it. When a waitress brought the food Dad handed her the sheet. "Give this to Mr. Stevens, will you, please?"

"Certainly." She took the note to Mr. Stevens who read it, then burst out laughing.

"You're on, Craig!" he said to Dad.

Everyone looked curiously from him to Dad. "What's that all about?" asked Mom curiously.

Dad grinned. "A private secret between Burt and me. Let's eat."

12

THE GAME Nick had dreaded was with the Tornadoes on Wednesday, July 27. He didn't like that smirk on Mr. Stevens's face. He didn't like Bugs Wheeler's sarcastic remarks. Matter of fact, he didn't like the Tornadoes at all.

"Let's beat these guys," he said as he squeezed in between Gale and Johnny on the bench. "We whipped them before. Let's do it again."

He wasn't starting at short. Jim Rennie was. That meant that he would go in for the last two or three innings.

"Bill, Jerry, Jim," Mom read off the

names of the first three hitters. "Pick up your bats. Get up there and swing."

The Thunderballs had first raps. Lefty Burns was pitching for the Tornadoes, looking tall and confident on the mound. He got two strikes on Bill, then Bill laced a grounder through short for a single, and went to second on Jerry's sacrifice bunt.

Jim flied out. Then Tom Warren doubled, scoring Bill, and Mike Todey singled, scoring Tom. Wayne flied out for the third out.

"Nice start, guys!" cried Nick as the guys came in for their gloves. "Now hold them."

The Tornadoes knocked in a run in the first and another one in the second. The Thunderballs crept ahead by one in the top of the third, but the Tornadoes picked up two to go into the lead 4 to 3.

"Hey, Nick!" shouted Bugs Wheeler.

"When are you guys going to buy your coach a uniform?"

"When you buy a muzzle for your mouth!" Nick yelled back. He wasn't going to let Bugs get away with every remark he made.

"That's telling him, Nick!" a Thunderball fan shouted.

Frankie Morrow, batting for Johnny Linn in the fourth, poled a long homer. Bill Dakes flied out. Then Gale, batting for Jerry, singled. And Nick, going in for Jim, drove a streaking grounder over the third-base sack for a double. The coach held Gale up at third. Scotty, pinch-hitting for Tom, flied out to deep short.

"Settle down, Lefty!" shouted a Tornadoes fan. "Smoke those pitches in there so they can't see 'em!"

He didn't smoke one past Mike Todey.

Mike singled through second, driving in both Gale and Nick. Then Wayne flied out for the second time. Three away.

The Tornadoes' bench was extremely quiet. Mr. Stevens looked concerned, and Bugs Wheeler seemed to have already purchased a muzzle and was wearing it. Nick grinned. Wouldn't it be something to beat the Tornadoes again? Then Mr. Stevens would think twice before considering the Thunderballs a pushover, and Bugs Wheeler's mouth would be muzzled for good.

The Tornadoes tied it up during their turn at bat, giving them, especially Bugs, an opportunity to blow their horns again. In the top of the fifth the Thunderballs failed to score. The Tornadoes came up and knocked in two to go into the lead 8 to 6.

"Come on, Nick!" the guys shouted as Nick stepped to the plate to lead off the last inning. "Start it off with a long blast!"

"You don't really think you'll do that, do you, Nick?" needled Bugs, smiling behind his face mask.

"Watch me," answered Nick.

Nick followed Lefty's first pitch carefully. Too low. The next one looked good. He swung. A long, clean, solid drive to deep left! The fans started to shout and whistle . . . even before the ball sailed over the fence!

"Were you watching?" Nick said to Bugs as he crossed the plate.

"Just lucky," Bugs mumbled.

"One more run ties it up!" Mom said excitedly. "Let's go after it, Scotty!"

Scotty tried. He singled. Mike flied out. Then Wayne singled, advancing Scotty to

second. That's where he stayed. Cyclone fanned and Pat popped up, ending the ball game. The Tornadoes won 8 to 7.

Outside of the Tornadoes' dugout Coach Stevens's face was beaming again. "Good game, Coach!" he yelled. "Gave us quite a battle!"

"Glad you thought so!" replied Mom, with that cool, unruffled smile of hers. You'd think the Thunderballs had won the game instead of the Tornadoes.

"I'd like to know what that secret is between you and Mr. Stevens, Dad," said Nick as they rode home in the car.

Dad grinned. "Sorry. A secret's a secret," he said.

Two days later the Thunderballs redeemed themselves by beating the Clowns.

Wayne and Scotty came over at eight

o'clock that evening and played with Nick's chess set in the tent. Wayne's family had returned from their cottage two days ago and Wayne seemed glad to be back. Guess he would rather be with a lot of friends than spend a vacation at a lake cottage with a boat, a surfboard, and probably all the ice cream and soda he could eat and drink.

Scotty easily beat Wayne the first game and also won the second, though not as easily. Nick, watching them play, was amused at how cautiously Wayne maneuvered his pawns and bishops. Chess was a game that took a lot of concentration and patience. Wayne was using both. In the third game Scotty still had several pawns left on the board when Wayne said, "Checkmate!"

Sure enough, he had Scotty blocked

from all directions. Then he challenged Nick. Nick beat him a game. By now it was getting dark and time for Wayne to go home.

"How about playing tomorrow?" Wayne asked.

"Sure. Come over in the afternoon. You've caught on pretty fast, Wayne. And you never played chess before?"

Wayne shook his head. "Never. It's a great game. I like it."

Wayne and Scotty went home and Nick went into the house. Mom was at the telephone. She seemed extremely concerned about something. Presently she hung up the receiver.

"What's the matter, Mom?" asked Jen. "What did Mrs. Maylor want?"

"She called to remind me that I'm in charge of the program at the Women's

Club at church on Tuesday night," said Mom, frowning thoughtfully. "It was planned so long ago that I had forgotten about it."

Nick went to the bulletin board where Mom tacked notes and looked at the baseball schedule. Next Tuesday the Thunderballs were playing the Knicks.

He turned to Mom, his face pale. "You didn't say you'd do it, did you, Mom? We're playing the Knicks on Tuesday."

She nodded. "I said yes, Nick. It's too late to back out now. It wouldn't be fair to make them find someone else at this late date."

He crumpled into a chair. Guess Mom was right. But you might as well consider that game lost even before it started.

13

DAD took over the coaching job on Tuesday against the Knicks. He quit work early purposely so he could. Johnny Linn pitched and had bad luck from the very start. He walked the first two men. Then an error by Nick gave the Knicks their first run.

The Knicks stretched their lead to five runs after picking up two in the second and two in the third. Monk Jones, hurling for them, seemed to do everything right. Trailing 5 to 0, the Thunderballs came alive in the top of the fourth and knocked in two runs. Dad's strategy to bunt Monk Jones as much as possible worked sometimes, but most of the Thunderballs weren't able to bunt well enough.

"We want Coach *Mrs.* Vassey!" a fan yelled. "Where's Coach *Mrs.* Vassey?"

Laughter started in the stands and presently the entire crowd had caught the laughter bug.

Nick smiled at Dad, who was taking it in good fun. "Guess they want Mom, Dad."

"So I hear. And I wish she were here. Believe me!"

In the top of the fifth the Knicks' shortstop missed Bill Dakes's skyscraping pop fly. Jerry Wong tripled, scoring Bill. But no one knocked Jerry in, and the score remained 5 to 3. In the bottom of the fifth an error by Gale in center field and an error by Cyclone at third helped the Knicks fill the bases.

"We want Coach *Mrs.* Vassey!" a fan yelled again. "Where's Coach *Mrs.* Vassey?"

"You think she could have kept those guys from making errors?" another fan piped up.

"No! But I think the boys play better for her than they do for her husband!" answered the first fan, and then roared with laughter. A dozen or so other fans burst out laughing, too.

"Mow 'em down, Johnny!" another Thunderball fan shouted. "Smoke that pill by 'em!"

The Knicks' batter watched the first pitch breeze past him for a called strike. He struck at the next one and met it solidly. A two-bagger that cleaned the bases.

The Knicks picked up another run before the Thunderballs managed to get them out. Knicks 9 — Thunderballs 3.

The Thunderballs rallied for two runs in the top of the sixth, but could get no more. The game went to the Knicks.

Mom had hardly entered the house that night when Sue yelled, "The Knicks trimmed the Thunderballs nine to five!"

"Quiet, Sue!" Nick glared at her. "Can't you let Mom get inside first before you give her that news?"

Mom looked at the faces around her. Her gaze finally settled on her husband. "We can't win them all, dear," she said and grinned at him.

Mom relaxed in an easy chair in the living room and told them about her program at the club. Nick and the girls filled her in on some of the things that had happened in the ball game. Dad seemed to have very little to add.

At nine-thirty the phone rang in the dining room. Jen set aside the book she was reading to answer it. "For you, Mom," she said.

"It's probably Mrs. Maylor," muttered Nick. "She probably wants Mom to run another program."

Nick tried to strain his ears to hear Mom's side of the conversation, but he couldn't. After a while Mom was back in the living room.

Mom looked at Nick. She was frowning. "That was Mrs. Snow," she said. "She and Mr. Snow just got home from seeing a play and Wayne isn't home. They had left the door open for him and he's been home. His uniform's there. But he is nowhere around and they're worried."

14

"I HAVEN'T seen him since the ball game," said Nick. "I don't know where he could've gone. He doesn't seem to have any other friends he visits."

"Even if he does, he should have gone home by now," said Dad.

"I'll call up Scotty and a couple of other guys," said Nick. "Maybe one of them has seen him."

He made the calls. Scotty said no, he didn't know where Wayne was. "How about me calling a couple guys and you calling a couple guys?" he suggested. "Then I'll call you back?"

"Good idea," replied Nick and they decided who to call. Neither of the guys Nick called knew where Wayne was. When Scotty called his news wasn't good either.

"Okay, thanks, Scotty."

"No luck," Nick said to Mom.

Dad looked at his wristwatch. "The Snows could call the local radio station and have them make an announcement that Wayne is missing."

"But the station's off the air," reminded Mom. "They sign off at eight o'clock."

"How about calling the police?" suggested Nick.

"No," said Dad. "That would be up to the Snows." He shook his head. "Wayne's never disappeared like this before, has he?"

"Not that I know of," said Nick. "I can't understand it."

And then a thought struck him. Chess. The tent. "That's a beauty," Wayne had said the first time he had seen it. "Ever spend a night in it?"

"Oh, sure," Nick remembered saying.

It was just possible . . . Without thinking further he put on a light jacket, got a flashlight and headed for the door.

"Nick, where are you going?" Dad asked.

"To the tent," answered Nick. "I'll be right back."

He closed the door softly behind him, then stole up to the tent, flashing the light ahead of him. He drew the flaps apart and looked inside. In the silence he heard soft

breathing. He turned the light toward the cot and caught his breath. There was Wayne Snow, stretched out under a blanket, fast asleep!

Nick went in and shook him. "Wayne! Get up!"

Wayne jerked awake. Nick turned the flashlight away so that the light wouldn't blind him. "I must've fallen asleep," murmured Wayne.

"I guess you did," replied Nick. "Your folks are looking for you."

Wayne flung the blanket aside and followed Nick out of the tent. There was a sound on the porch and Nick saw Mom and Dad standing there.

"He's here," said Nick. "He was sleeping in the tent."

"Gracious!" cried Mom, and clattered down the steps in her slippers. "You've given a lot of people quite a scare, Wayne. Why did you do a thing like that and not say anything?"

"I didn't mean to fall asleep. I just wanted to be here awhile, is all."

"Your mother and father are dreadfully worried about you."

"Yeah, I bet."

Mom frowned. "What?"

"Nothing."

Mom and Dad looked at each other. Then Mom put an arm around Wayne's shoulders. "Come on. I'll drive you home."

"Good night, Wayne," said Nick.

"Good night, Nick," Wayne answered.

15

ON Friday, August 5, the Thunderballs played the Zebras. The sky
was cloudy and getting darker every minute. A storm was brewing in the west.

The teams played four innings before
the rain came and halted everything. Fans
scattered out of the park to their cars or
whatever shelter they could find. The
Thunderballs and the Zebras sought the
shelter of their dugouts.

After a while the base and plate umpires
got together, discussed the situation and
called off the game. Since it had gone at

least four innings, the Thunderballs, leading 7 to 3, were declared the winners.

On August 11 they played the Tornadoes for the third time, not counting the practice game. It was the Tornadoes' last game of the season. Tomorrow's game between the Thunderballs and the Clowns would be the last for the Thunderballs.

The Tornadoes had beaten the Zebras on Wednesday, leaving them with a record of six wins and five losses. Up till today the Thunderballs' record was seven wins and three losses. If they beat the Tornadoes today they would clinch the pennant.

If! A small word, thought Nick. But it meant so much!

From the Tornadoes' dugout Coach Stevens was watching his star hurler, Lefty Burns, warming up. Now and then he glanced toward the Thunderballs' bench. Could it be that he was worried?

Nick grinned and looked at Mom. She was in the dugout, writing up the batting order. It was hard to tell whether she was nervous.

After a while the Tornadoes infielders took their practice and then the Thunderballs took theirs. A few minutes later the ball game began.

The crowd was the largest Nick had seen at the park. He stood by the dugout and watched, hoping to see the Snows. But in the sea of faces it was almost impossible to recognize anyone.

Frankie Morrow, on the mound for the Thunderballs, took his time. The infielders were giving him all the verbal support they could. "Down the groove, Frankie!"

"Breeze it by 'im, Frankie!"

"The old go, kid! Let's get 'em outa there!"

Frankie toed the rubber, stretched, delivered. A bunt down the third-base line! Pat seemed to be taken by surprise; he started after the ball too late. By the time he got it and pegged to first, the runner was there. The Tornado was given a hit.

"Let's wake up, boys!" shouted Mom, sitting beside Nick in the dugout. "Keep on your toes!"

Nick looked toward the Tornadoes' dugout. Just as he thought . . . nearly the entire Tornadoes' bench was laughing.

"You tell 'em, Coach!" Bugs Wheeler yelled. "They'll need it!'

Another bunt! And again toward third! Pat, playing in, fielded it. He started to throw to second, saw that he might not get the runner, then pegged to first. Out!

The next hitter drove a hard grounder to short. Jim fielded it, pegged to first. Two outs!

123

The next hitter tagged a long one to left center that went for a double, scoring the runner. Frankie struck the next man out.

Jerry Wong was the only one who managed to get a hit in the bottom of the inning. He died on second. The Tornadoes picked up another run when they came to bat.

"A run an inning!" yelled Bugs Wheeler. "That's enough to beat the Thunderballs!"

"Can't someone knock a foul ball right square into his big mouth?" muttered Scotty.

Mom laughed. "Let him enjoy himself, Scotty. Our laugh will come. Remember, 'He who laughs last . . .' "

" 'Laughs best,' " finished Scotty.

"Or 'longest.' "

Wayne led off. He took a called strike, then two balls. Then he leaned into a low pitch and drove it solidly toward deep left field. It kept going . . . going . . . going . . . A home run!

The smile on Wayne's face as he crossed the plate was the first real one Nick had seen in a long time. The guys gripped his hand. The fans cheered and clapped.

"Okay. The ice is broken," Mom said. "Let's keep it cracking."

Russ hit a high one that pierced the sky then came down only to be caught by the second baseman. Pat beat out a slow grounder to short, bringing up Frankie who got a loud hand from the fans. Frankie fouled two pitches, then fanned for out number two. Bill laced a double over the second baseman's head, scoring Pat. Then Jerry flied out. The score was tied at 2 all.

The Tornadoes' lead-off man tried to

bunt the first pitch and missed. He took a ball, then hit a hard grounder back at Frankie. Frankie tossed the ball to first for an easy out. The next batter hit a high foul ball over Wayne's head. Wayne caught it. A hit and an error put two men on, but Frankie struck out the next man for the third out.

"What happened to that run an inning, Bugsy?" Nick yelled across to the Tornado catcher.

Bugs smiled. "Don't worry! We'll pick it up the next time!"

Jim led off in the bottom of the third. A Texas leaguer over short! Then Tom Warren laid into Lefty Burns's first pitch and drilled it to right center, scoring Jim. Nick, in the coaching box at third, held Tom up at the third-base sack. Mike struck out.

"Another blast, Wayne!" the fans shouted as Wayne came to bat.

He blasted one, a high fly to center field. The fielder stepped back three steps and pulled it in. Tom tagged up, then ran in to score. Russ flied out for the second time. Three away. But they had gone ahead by two runs.

"Okay, Nick," said Mom. "Take short in place of Jim. Gale, take center field. Scotty, left field. Cyclone, third base. And *hold* them."

16

COACH Stevens was standing outside of the dugout, his voice booming above those of the crowd. "Come on, Tommy! You're better than he is! Get on, boy!"

Tommy got on.

Mom shouted to Cyclone at third base to play in on the grass in case of a bunt. But the next hitter didn't bunt. He laced a pitch between third and short for a single, advancing the runner to second. The third hitter socked a hard grounder to Nick. Nick fumbled it, then retrieved it in time to throw out the man at third. One away. Men on first and second.

Frankie rubbed the ball, then lifted off his cap and wiped his forehead with the sleeve of his jersey. It was a scorching hot day. Clouds lay like tattered strings across the sky. Many of the fans wore dark glasses. Those who didn't squinted against the sunlight.

Frankie toed the rubber, nodded at the signal from Wayne, then stretched and delivered. The ball breezed in belt-high and the batter swung. The blow was solid. The ball sailed over second, heading for the vacant space between right and center fields. It was good for three bases. The Tornadoes couldn't knock the man in but they had evened the score, 4 to 4.

Nick didn't want to look toward the Tornadoes' bench, but he couldn't help it.

Bugs Wheeler had just said something to Coach Stevens and was laughing as if it were very funny.

The Thunderballs banged out two hits against Lefty during their turn at bat, but could not score. The Tornadoes came to bat in the top of the fifth and started to hit Frankie all over the lot.

Nick looked at Mom. What was she waiting for? The Tornadoes to get 16 runs off him?

"Mom!" he shouted and turned red as he realized that he must have been heard all over the diamond. Laughter rippled from the fans.

A run scored. A man walked. Another one hit.

"For crying out loud, Mom!" This time he hardly cared.

"Nick! Stop yelling at her like that! She knows what she's doing!"

The strong voice came from behind him. Nick turned and looked at Gale Matson.

"Yell all you want, Nick," said Gale. "But not at your mom. You'll just shake her up. Leave her alone."

The words sank into Nick and bit a little, made him think. Gale was right. He had no business yelling at Mom like that. And how many kids' mothers would have the courage to take on a coaching job? Nick realized that he was quite proud of Mom.

The Tornadoes scored another run, and then Mom took Frankie out and put in Johnny Linn. There were two on and one away. A tough spot for Johnny.

He pitched to the first hitter and struck him out amid loud cheers from the fans. "One more, Johnny!" his teammates yelled. "One more!"

A line drive over short! A run scored!

The next man flied out, ending the half-inning. Tornadoes 7 — Thunderballs 4.

"What I hate to see worst of all is the Tornadoes' winning the pennant again this year," snorted Scotty as he sat down.

"Don't give up hope," advised Mom confidently. "Even if we lose today we can still win the pennant by winning tomorrow. Pick up a bat and hustle to the plate, Scotty. You're first hitter."

"Start it off, Scotty," said Nick. "I'd like to bat this inning."

Scotty waited out the pitches, then smashed a single through second base. Mike glanced over his shoulder at Mom, then strode to the plate. Mom must have given him the bunt sign because he laid the first pitch down the third-base line for a perfect bunt. The third baseman was caught flat-footed, but the pitcher fielded the ball and threw Mike out.

Nick stared at Mom. "Aren't we too far behind to bunt?" he asked. She couldn't have used her noodle on that play. Teams usually did not bunt when they were three runs behind and there was only one more inning to go.

Mom tapped his knee gently. "Do we have to do the expected all the time?" she said. "Mike hasn't been hitting. He's popped up and struck out his first two times up. I was hoping he could have fooled the Tornadoes enough to get on, too."

Gale, sitting at Nick's other side, shoved his knee against Nick's. "What did I tell you? She knows what she's doing. Just leave her alone."

Mom laughed. "Why thanks, Gale!" she said.

Wayne, his shoulders wet from perspiration, stepped to the plate. He had hom-

ered the first time up and had socked a sacrifice fly the second time. He took a called strike, a ball, another ball, then swung. A grass-cutting grounder through the mound that just missed Lefty's legs! The hit went for two bases, scoring Scotty.

Russ smashed a single over the second baseman's head, and the Thunderball fans stood up and cheered as Wayne scored.

"One more run and it's tied up! Keep the rally going!" shouted Mom.

Cyclone, who had flied out in the fourth inning, flied out again. He seemed so disappointed he shook his head all the way back to the dugout.

"Cheer up, Cyclone," said Nick. "You'll have another chance next inning."

Johnny walked and the head of the line-up was up again — Bill Dakes. He belted a hit over the third-base sack. Russ scored from second. The coach halted Johnny at third. Again the fans went wild. The game was tied up!

"A hit, Gale!" they shouted. "A hit!"

But Gale Matson flied out.

"Just hold them," pleaded Mom. "Just *hold* them!"

The Thunderballs held the Tornadoes. One out. Two outs. And then the Tornadoes began to hit. A double. A single. And then a triple — before the Thunderballs could get them out.

"The game isn't over yet," said Mom. "Nick, get on."

Nick led off. Two runs behind, he thought. They needed three to win. Possible, but not probable.

The pitch. He swung. A long, long drive! The ball was reaching for the sky in left field! The crowd was screaming. And then the ball disappeared . . . over the fence!

"The old powerhouse, himself," smiled Gale as Nick came running in. "Too bad there weren't men on."

Scotty flied out to left. Mike doubled, Wayne walked. But that was it. Russ fanned and Cyclone flied out again. The Tornadoes took the game 9 to 8.

Now the Tornadoes had a chance at the pennant. They had seven wins and five losses and the Thunderballs had seven wins, four losses with one more game to play. Nick realized that if they lost to the Clowns on Friday, the Thunderballs and Tornadoes would be tied at six and six and would tangle again in a play-off.

17

"A REAL good game, Coach," Coach Stevens said to Mom, with that broad, amused smile of his. Nick watched them shake hands.

"At least we gave the fans their money's worth, didn't we?" Mom said. Her eyes were sparkling but Nick could tell she wasn't as happy as she looked. It would have been great to have knocked off the Tornadoes.

"You still have tomorrow's game to play," said Coach Stevens. "Naturally I can't wish you luck in it."

"Naturally," Mom echoed. "For if we win, we also win the pennant. And you wouldn't want *me* — a woman who's coaching for the first time in her life — to do *that,* would you?"

Coach Stevens chuckled. "Well, I'm looking forward to that play-off."

Dad came up beside them. "All I can say, Coach Vassey, is that you win that game tomorrow, or else."

Mom beamed up at him. "And all I can say, Mr. Vassey, is let's wait and see."

It seemed that all the parents of both teams were attending the Clowns-Thunderballs game the next day, Friday, plus most of the people of Flat Rock. Gale Matson's parents were there. So were Wayne Snow's. Nick looked twice at the Snows to see if he was right. Yes, they were the Snows, all right. Mr. and Mrs. Snow and

Ron. They were sitting halfway up the stands behind the third-base dugout, the dugout which today belonged to the Thunderballs.

The Clowns, batting first, could do nothing against Johnny Linn that first inning. A walk, a flyout, and then two singles in succession gave the Thunderballs a one-run lead. Nick, sitting it out until Mom put him in, watched Stinky Morrison carefully. Stinky, the Clowns' left-handed pitcher, had always worried Nick. He wished the Thunderballs would pile up a heap of runs before he went in.

The Clowns picked up two in the top of the second as a result of two errors, one by Jim at short and another by first baseman Russ Gray.

"I hope they get *that* out of their system right now," Mom said.

The Thunderballs scored a zero at their turn at bat. So did the Clowns in the top of the third. Then, in the bottom of the third, the Thunderballs cut loose. Jerry Wong started it with a double. Jim and Tom both got out. But Mike tagged a high pitch for two bases, scoring Jerry. And Wayne blasted a long triple to the left-field fence, scoring Mike.

Nick, coaching at third, looked behind him and saw the Snows clapping and cheering like teen-agers. Wayne, at third, looked as sober-faced as if hitting triples were something he did all the time. Russ knocked him in, Pat flied out and that was the end of the third inning.

The Clowns came back strong as ever. Nick, playing shortstop now, muffed a hot grounder that bounded off at a crazy angle and permitted the hitter to get two bases.

Then a home run got the Clowns' fans yelling like a bunch of hyenas.

"Hey, Nick!" Jabber Kane shouted from the third-base coaching box. "Who's going to coach the Thunderballs next year? Your aunt?"

"This game isn't over yet, Jabber!" Nick shouted back.

They scored another run before the Thunderballs could stop them. Clowns 5 — Thunderballs 4.

Johnny led off with a double in the bottom of the fourth. Cyclone, pinch-hitting for Bill, rapped out a single. Pat, now coaching at third, windmilled Johnny home. Then Jerry hit into a double play and Nick struck out.

In the fifth the Clowns roared again. This time Gale fumbled a fly ball in left field, letting in a run. It drew a disappointed moan from the crowd, but a sadder one from Gale. Nick could hear him from short. The Clowns scored twice more to advance into the lead 8 to 5.

"Hey, you Thunderballs!" cried a voice from the stands. "Why don't you throw in your gloves and quit now before you get slaughtered?"

Nick and several other guys looked up. Sure enough it was Bugs Wheeler and five or six other players from the Tornadoes. Not far from them sat Coach Burt Stevens, grinning triumphantly. They clearly had come with hopes of seeing the Clowns whip the Thunderballs. Then the Tornadoes and Thunderballs would be tied for the pennant.

It looked as if their hopes were going to come true. Stinky held the Thunderballs to a double in the bottom of the fifth, and no runs.

The Clowns started off well again as

they came up for the sixth and final inning. Cyclone let a grounder zip through his legs. That was it, though. The Clowns couldn't score.

"One, two, three, Stinky!" yelled Bugs Wheeler.

"Dog!" snorted Nick.

Pat, leading off, flied out. Johnny walked. Cyclone flied out. One more out and the ball game would be over.

Then Jerry singled. They were still alive! "Keep it going, Nick!" Mom shouted.

"Save me a rap, Nick!" Gale Matson pleaded.

Nick looked nervously at Stinky. For some unknown reason he was never able to hit Stinky's pitches. He was sure that if he swung away he'd strike out, just as he had done the last time. And that would be it. The ball game would be over, and Bugs

Wheeler, Coach Stevens and the rest of the Tornadoes would never let him live it down. They'd be gloating at the play-off game.

Suddenly he remembered what Mom had said in another game: *Do we have to do the expected all the time?* He looked toward first and then third. The Clowns were playing deep. He could try a bunt. It just might work. What could he lose?

The pitch came in. He shifted his feet and bunted the ball down the third-base line, catching the Clowns completely off their guard! The bunt was perfect!

"Nice going, Nick!" shouted Mom.

Three on and Gale came up. The fans yelled. Gale's parents sat still, waiting patiently.

"There you are, Gale!" yelled Nick. "I saved you a rap! Now, clonk it!"

Stinky stretched and pitched. Gale

swung. *Crack!* A solid smash! A high long ball to deep left! It kept going . . . going . . . Gone over the fence! A home run!

It was over. The Thunderballs — and Mom — had won the pennant.

Gale beamed proudly as he gripped Nick's hand. "Thanks for saving me that rap!"

The Snows came forward and shook hands with Mom. "Wayne thinks an awful lot of you, Mrs. Vassey," said Mrs. Snow. "He's always talking about you and your family. I wonder if you all would come over some day soon. My husband and I would love to have you. Will you?"

Mom's face shone radiantly. "We'll be glad to, Mrs. Snow."

Another figure joined the small group. Burt Stevens. A smile was on his face but it wasn't as broad as it had been. He stretched out his hand to shake Mom's.

"Congratulations, Coach," he said. "You won it fair and square."

Mom's eyes sparkled. "Thank you, Mr. Stevens," she said, and then added mischievously, "Sorry you don't get a chance for a play-off."

"And I won the bet," Dad said. "The Stevenses are taking the Vasseys out for a Chinese dinner. That's the bet we had agreed on in Mr. Wong's restaurant. Tomorrow okay, Coach Stevens?"

"Tomorrow's fine," smiled Mr. Stevens.

How many of these Matt Christopher sports classics have you read?

Baseball
- ☐ Baseball Pals
- ☐ Catcher with a Glass Arm
- ☐ The Diamond Champs
- ☐ The Fox Steals Home
- ☐ The Kid Who Only Hit Homers
- ☐ Look Who's Playing First Base
- ☐ Miracle at the Plate
- ☐ No Arm in Left Field
- ☐ Shortstop from Tokyo
- ☐ The Year Mom Won the Pennant

Basketball
- ☐ Johnny Long Legs
- ☐ Long Shot for Paul

Dirt Bike Racing
- ☐ Dirt Bike Racer
- ☐ Dirt Bike Runaway

Football
- ☐ Catch That Pass!
- ☐ The Counterfeit Tackle
- ☐ Football Fugitive
- ☐ Tight End
- ☐ Touchdown for Tommy
- ☐ Tough to Tackle

Ice Hockey
- ☐ Face-Off
- ☐ Ice Magic

Soccer
- ☐ Soccer Halfback

Track
- ☐ Run, Billy, Run

All available in paperback from Little, Brown and Company